TAKE TO THE SKIES

SUPER HUMAN

TAKE TO THE SKIES

R. T. MARTIN

darby creek

MINNEAPOLIS

Darby Creek
A division of Lerner Publishing Group, Inc.
241 First Avenue North
Minneapolis, MN 55401 USA

For reading levels and more information, look up this title at www.lernerbooks.com.

The images in this book are used with the permission of: © iStockphoto.com/Vladimirovic; © iStockphoto.com/aarrows; © iStockphoto.com/johan63; © iStockphoto.com/DWalker44; © iStockphoto.com/Maxiphoto; © iStockphoto.com/sinemaslow.

Main body text set in Janson Text LT Std 12/17.5.
Typeface provided by Adobe Systems.

Library of Congress Cataloging-in-Publication Data

Names: Martin, R. T., 1988– author.
Title: Take to the skies / by R.T. Martin.
Description: Minneapolis : Darby Creek, [2018] | Series: Superhuman | Summary: On her sixteenth birthday, Cassie discovers that she has the power of flight, an ability she wants to keep secret from her parents and friends, but when disaster strikes she must make a difficult choice.
Identifiers: LCCN 2017004655 (print) | LCCN 2017031799 (ebook) | ISBN 9781512498387 (eb pdf) | ISBN 9781512498271 (lb : alk. paper)
Subjects: | CYAC: Flight—Fiction. | Ability—Fiction. | Secrets—Fiction. | High schools—Fiction. | Schools—Fiction. | Family life—Fiction.
Classification: LCC PZ7.1.M37346 (ebook) | LCC PZ7.1.M37346 Tak 2018 (print) | DDC [Fic]—dc23

LC record available at https://lccn.loc.gov/2017004655

Manufactured in the United States of America
1-43578-33359-6/5/2017

For Anna Weggel-Reed

SIXTEEN YEARS AGO, ON APRIL 12, SIX PEOPLE FROM AROUND THE COUNTRY WERE BORN WITH A HIDDEN SPECIAL ABILITY.

On their sixteenth birthday, they each develop their special ability for the first time. Whether they can soar through the clouds, run faster than the speed of light, or tear through a brick wall, all the teenagers must choose how to use their powers. Will they keep their abilities secret? Will they use them only to benefit themselves? Or will they attempt to help others—even if the risks are greater than they could imagine? One way or another, each teen will have to learn what it means to be . . . superhuman.

1

Bzzz Bzzz Bzzz

Cassie pulled her phone out of her pocket. Keeping it below her desk so Ms. Talin wouldn't see it, she looked at the three text messages she just received. They were in the group thread she had with her two best friends, Nikki and Mario. The first was from Nikki, who was sitting right behind her in class. It read, *BIRTHDAY GIRL! SWEET 16!!!* The next was from Mario and read, *HAPPY BIRTHDAY!!!* The third was also from Mario—just a series of penguin emojis that he sent whenever he wanted to show he was happy or excited.

Cassie turned around and smiled at her friend. Nikki excitedly smiled back at her.

"Pay attention, Cassie," came Ms. Talin's voice suddenly. Cassie faced forward. "Now, as I was saying, *this*,"—she gestured to an egg placed in front of her on a lab table—"is a standard egg, and *this*,"—she pulled a flat cylinder out of her pocket—"is a three-pound weight."

Ms. Talin gently placed the weight on top of the egg, adjusting it slightly until it was balanced before letting go. The egg didn't break. Instead the weight just stayed balanced on top of it. "Who can tell me why the egg isn't broken?"

Nikki raised her hand, and Ms. Talin pointed to her. "Three pounds isn't enough to break an egg."

"Sure it is," Ms. Talin replied, as if she'd been expecting that exact response. She picked up the weight and dropped it on the egg. This time it exploded, spewing the inside in all directions. Several students around Cassie flinched backward or shielded their face from the flying globs of egg.

"See?" Ms. Talin said, wiping some yolk off her blazer. "Three pounds breaks an egg easily."

"Well, yeah, but only if you drop it," a student across the room said.

"That's right," Ms. Talin said. "Who can tell me why dropping the weight makes a difference?"

"A moving object has more force than one that's standing still," the same student answered.

"Exactly," Ms. Talin said, walking around the lab table. "An eggshell can withstand about three point seven five pounds of force, but when I drop the weight, three pounds becomes more than three pounds because of gravity. The weight is being pulled toward Earth's center. That adds force. Why am I telling you this?" She opened a carton of eggs and showed them to the class. "Because each of you will have to drop one of these eggs off the roof of this building for this year's school-wide science challenge. Each science class is taking a time-out from the regular curriculum to do this project, but it still counts as part of your grade in this class. Your job is to make sure that your egg doesn't break."

Some kids groaned, some laughed, and one student said, "We get to go on the roof?"

"You'll be working in teams of two, so pick a partner—and yes, you'll get to go on the roof the day of the experiment."

Two students said, "Nice!" in unison. Nikki poked Cassie in the back. She turned around. "Partners?" Nikki asked.

"Partners," Cassie said as the bell rang.

At the end of the day, Cassie and Nikki waited in front of the school for Mario as usual.

"Happy birthday, Cass!" he shouted as soon as he saw them.

Cassie laughed. "You've said that to me every time you've seen me today, Mario. Nice penguins, by the way."

Nikki and Mario had been friends since they were little, but Cassie had just met Nikki in their biology class this year and getting to know Mario had kind of come hand in hand with befriending Nikki. Mario, it turned out, lived across the street from Cassie, and Nikki lived only a few blocks from there, so the three of them had been walking home together every day since the fall.

A few blocks from home, Cassie made sure they were going to make it to her place for her birthday celebration that night. Nikki planned to head over right after she finished her homework. Mario was going to come by after he destroyed the snake of Agathor, which Cassie assumed was a monster in one of his fantasy video games. She laughed and wished him luck in battle.

"In battle, there is no luck—only skill and determination," he said.

At home, the apartment was empty. Her eleven-year-old brother, Danny, would get home in about ten minutes. Cassie checked the whiteboard on the refrigerator door, where her mom and dad usually left notes, but there was nothing there. That meant they were either at work or looking at a house. They'd been going to open houses for about three months now, and Cassie was beginning to wonder if they were ever going to actually buy one.

Cassie tossed her bag onto her desk chair and lay down on her bed. She started thinking about the science project. *We could build a little parachute*, she thought, *or what if we put it in a bag full of cotton balls?* Even though science was far from her favorite subject, this particular project had grabbed Cassie's interest. *It's basically problem-solving*, she thought. *It could actually be kind of fun.*

She closed her eyes and began to drift off. She was startled awake by the sound of the front door closing. Just as she woke, for a brief moment, she had that feeling like she was about to fall off the bed. *I must have been more tired than I thought.*

"Cass?" her brother shouted from the entryway.

"I'm in my room."

He poked his head through the doorway. "How's your birthday so far?"

She smiled. "Not bad. Go do some homework until Mom and Dad get home."

"Can I have the TV on?" he asked. Cassie knew he wanted to watch the new show based on his favorite comic book, *Altitude*, about a superhero who could fly. Danny had always loved superhero cartoons and showed no signs of outgrowing his obsession any time soon.

"Fine," she said, "but don't let it distract you." As Danny headed out to the living room, she thought about how excited she was that Mario and Nikki were coming over to celebrate with her.

This was bound to be better than last year's birthday, which she spent by herself after she found out her previous group of friends had planned a spring break trip without her. She'd only heard about the trip when she tried to invite everyone to come over and they finally admitted that they would be gone over her birthday. Her parents had offered to take her out for a celebration dinner, but she was so upset after learning that her friends didn't want to hang out with her anymore that she'd locked herself in her bedroom for the entire night.

That doesn't matter anymore though, Cassie reminded herself. She had her new friends. They were going to come over for a birthday dinner made by her parents, followed by her mom's famous caramel and dark chocolate cake, and Cassie figured they'd top the night off with one of her favorite old movies. It was exactly what Cassie wanted—simple, but still a great birthday.

***

Pretty good haul this year, Cassie thought to herself later that night. Nikki had given her a cookbook from their local bookstore, and Mario had given her a poster of her favorite hockey team, signed by the goalie. She'd been thrilled about the new cell phone from her parents too. Secretly, though, she liked Mario's gift the most. Cassie went to bed happy and fell asleep as soon as her head hit the pillow.

The dream came suddenly and vividly. She was soaring over buildings. She could go as high as she wanted and knew that she wouldn't fall. She'd had dreams like this before—they were her favorite, so much fun and so incredibly thrilling. She swooped rapidly between the buildings downtown, looking down on the people who all seemed so tiny from this height. She flew in spirals and loops, chasing birds that couldn't go as fast as she could.

Cassie's eyes shot open, and she could feel cold sweat all over her body. She looked at her alarm clock—3:00 a.m. The dream had been so vivid and realistic that waking up from it had actually startled her. She tried to sit up, but when she went to put her hands on the bed to push herself upward, there was nothing there. She looked down. The bed was about four feet below her. She was floating in midair.

2

Cassie tried to grab onto her bed, but it was beyond her reach. *What is happening?!*

Just then, she slammed back down onto the bed with a thud. She bolted upright and tried to wrap her mind around what just happened.

I was floating, she thought. *I was really floating.* She sat for a bit, breathing heavily. *No, I couldn't have been floating. That's impossible. It must have just been my dream, or that stupid show Danny is always watching. I was flying in my dream, and when I woke up, my mind was playing tricks on me.* She lay back down and repeated that the floating had just been part of her dream. Eventually she calmed down and was able to fall back asleep.

When she woke the next morning, she was positive that the whole incident had just been part of the dream. She got dressed and went into the kitchen. Her parents were cooking breakfast and chattering about house showings.

"That one's way out of our price range," her mom said.

Her dad shrugged. "Maybe they'll accept a little less for it."

"The realtor said they already had one offer at the asking price and they'll probably get another one soon."

"Well, that one's out then," her dad said as he slid eggs onto Cassie's plate. "Maybe we'll have better luck at the showing tonight."

"Oh, that reminds me," her mom said, turning to Cassie. "You're in charge of Danny this evening. We won't be back until about eight, but there are some leftovers in the fridge if you get hungry before then."

"Okay," Cassie replied. "On your way home, can you pick up some more eggs? Nikki and I have a science project. We have to drop an egg off the roof of the school and make sure it doesn't break."

"Need to have a few test runs, eh?" her dad said, leaning on the counter and taking a sip of coffee. "No problem."

Danny came out of his room, scarfed down his breakfast before Cassie had a chance to finish hers, and declared that he was ready to leave. Cassie finished her eggs, stuffed her books into her backpack, and left with her little brother. She often thought it would be great to walk *to* school with her best friends, but Nikki had swim practice an hour before school began, and Mario—well, Mario was never on time.

At lunch, Nikki and Cassie brainstormed ways to prevent their egg from breaking. Mario sat down next to them and handed Cassie a note with a hand drawn penguin doodle. This time the penguin had a speaking bubble that said, "Happy day after your birthday!" It made Cassie laugh. Nikki rolled her eyes.

"What if we just stuffed the egg into a pillow?" Nikki asked.

"I don't think there's enough stuffing in a pillow," Cassie replied, taking a bite out of her sandwich. "I think the parachute is our best bet."

"What if, instead of letting it drop," Mario said, "you built a little jetpack, so it just keeps going up? If it never hits the ground, it doesn't break."

"Have I ever told you how helpful you are?" Nikki asked.

"No."

"Well," she said with a smile, "there's a reason."

They continued brainstorming ideas through the rest of the lunch period. The day went by faster than usual. Before long, Cassie was home. After tossing her bag on the chair in her bedroom, she lay on the bed and was reminded of the floating incident that happened last night. *It was just a dream*, she reminded herself, *but it felt so real. I could have sworn I was floating. What if I really was—*

Her train of thought was cut off by the front door closing and her brother shouting, "Cass?"

She came out of her room. "Yeah, I'm here. Mom and Dad said they won't be home until about eight, so I'm in charge tonight."

Danny dropped his bag on the kitchen table. "Can we go up on the roof?"

"No!" she fired back. Their apartment building had a community patio area through the roof access stairs.

"Why not?"

"Because you go too close to the ledge, and one of these days, you're going to fall off of it." Danny was constantly peeking over the ledge whenever they went up there. It made Cassie nervous every time. He would play a game where he would see how far he could lean over the ledge without falling. He hadn't lost the game yet, but it was a dangerous one to be playing. Cassie hated it.

"I won't go near the ledge," he insisted. "I just want to do my homework up there. The weather's so nice now, and it's cool being on the roof."

"Not happening," Cassie said, crossing her arms.

"Pleeeaaase?"

"No."

"Pleeeaaase?"

"No."

"Pleeeaaase?"

"Fine!" she blurted out. She knew he'd keep at this for hours if that's what it took. "But you really do have to stay away from the ledge."

"Okay!" He picked up his backpack and headed to the door.

"Wait for me. You're not allowed to go up by yourself." Cassie grabbed her bag from her room and met her brother at the front door. They went up the six flights of stairs to the roof access door.

There was a picnic area up there with a few benches and tables and a grill. None of their neighbors seemed to have much interest in the roof, but Danny *loved* it. Whenever the weather was even moderately nice, he wanted to go up. Danny was just like that boy who got excited when he heard that the students would get to go on the school roof to drop their eggs.

They sat at a bench and each began their homework. After about an hour, Danny was finished and started reading his newest *Altitude* comic book. Cassie was concentrating on a math formula when she heard some rustling around and looked up to see Danny next to the edge of the roof.

She slammed her book shut. "Seriously, Danny! What did I say about going near the ledge?"

"I'm just looking," he said.

"I don't care what you're doing. Get away from there!"

"Relax. I'm not going to fall."

"Danny, come back here right now!"

Danny pretended not to hear her, as he usually did when he played this game. Instead, he climbed up onto the ledge. She knew he was deliberately trying to make her mad now. "Don't do that—you're going to fall! Get back over to this bench right now, or I'm telling Mom and Dad when they get home!"

He ignored her again. Now he was standing on the ledge.

"Danny, if you don't—" It wasn't until Cassie's textbook suddenly fell off her lap that she noticed something felt wrong. She looked down and saw that the bench she had just been sitting on was now several feet below her. She pivoted in the air and tried to grab onto it, but just like her bed had been the previous night, it was out of reach.

"No, no, no, no," she said in a panic.

"See, I told you I wouldn't—" Danny started, but he'd turned around and saw Cassie floating. His eyes went wide. Out of shock, he tried to take a step back, but his foot caught on the lip of the ledge. He tumbled backward and out of sight.

3

"Danny!" Cassie shouted. Suddenly she was flying off the roof. She swooped down the side of the building fast enough to make her stomach churn and reached her brother. She grabbed at his hand and pulled him closer to her.

Before she could really think about what she was doing, she had stopped their fall so they were hanging in midair.

For a moment, they hung there, staring at and grasping each other. They were floating twenty feet below the ledge of the roof—Danny below Cassie, gripping her hand as tight as he could.

Cassie looked up at the roof. First she tried to grab onto a window ledge, but they were too far away from the building. She tried to thrust herself up but only made it about five feet before they were just hovering again. She pushed herself upward, like trying to rise to the top of a pool, again and again and again, but it was difficult with Danny's weight pulling her downward.

After a few repetitions, Cassie got her hand on the ledge and, using all of her strength, pulled Danny up until he could grab onto it too. They both crawled over the lip and rolled onto the gravel of the rooftop.

When they were both safe, Cassie rolled over and lay faceup. She felt as if she'd just run a marathon. Her face was hot and beaded with sweat. She could feel her pulse in her temples and had to control her breathing to calm down as she looked up at the sky.

"How—how—how did you do that?" Danny sat up, looking down at her as he too struggled to catch his breath.

"I don't know," she said, panting.

"Are you wearing ropes or something?" Danny started waving his hands through the air around her, as if trying to figure out how his sister had pulled off such an elaborate magic trick.

"No, I'm not attached to any ropes. I was—I don't know. It was like a reflex. When I saw you fall, I just—I don't know."

"You were flying," Danny said. "You were actually *flying*. Since when can you fly?"

Now that she'd caught her breath, Cassie stood up. "Just since yesterday. I started hovering, but I wasn't trying to. It just sort of happens. I didn't know I could—I didn't know I could do *that*."

Danny was smiling so wide his lips were nearly touching his ears. "This—is—awesome! You can fly! Do you realize what this means? You're just like Altitude! You could fly over to England right now if you wanted! Hey, can I get on your back, and you could fly us—"

Cassie put up a hand and cut him off. "Okay, one, I'm not an amusement park ride. Two, I can't—I'm not some kind of . . . flying person. I've only hovered before, and I don't even know how I did that. Three, even if I could, the last thing I'd do is start zipping around the city where anyone could see me. I don't—I don't want people to know I can do . . . this."

"Why?" Danny asked. "What's the worst that could happen?"

"A lot!" Cassie fired back. "The government could lock me up and do experiments on me."

"Are you serious? The government has more important things to do, Cass. I don't think anybody can legally lock you up unless you commit a crime."

He had a point. Was she overreacting? "But . . . but . . ." Cassie struggled to put her fear into words. "Everyone would start treating me like I'm—like I'm different." Being different had been what caused her old friends to ditch her in the first place—they thought she wasn't cool enough. She'd been trying to seem normal for Mario and Nikki, but *this*? How could she possibly explain this away as normal?

"But you *are* different!" Danny said. "Like it or not. Hey, if I'm related to you, do you think that when I turn sixteen I'll be able to—"

"I don't want to be different!" Cassie cut him off again.

"Well," Danny said, "tough luck. What does it feel like when you do it?"

Cassie tried to remember. The whole thing had happened in a sort of blur. She'd just panicked when Danny fell of the roof. She hadn't been paying attention to how she'd done it, but when she thought back to what just occurred, there was no way to deny it any longer. "It's hard to explain," she said. "I guess it's sort of like flexing a muscle. When I was pulling you up, I sort of pushed my body in the direction I wanted to go."

"Pushed off of what?"

"Nothing. I don't know, Danny. I already said it's hard to explain." She looked at her brother who was still grinning back at her. This must have been a sort of dream come true for him. He read so many of those *Altitude* comics and watched so many superhero shows that to know a real person with an ability like this must have been thrilling to him. "Don't tell Mom and Dad," she said.

"Why not?"

"Because I don't want them to know." She paused for a moment. "I don't want them to send me away or something."

Danny scrunched up his face. "You really think they would do that?"

"No," she admitted. "But, still . . . you know what I mean. I just don't want anyone else to know."

"Okay," he said, "I won't tell Mom and Dad on one condition." Cassie raised an eyebrow. "You have to learn how to control it."

"Control what?" she asked.

"Your power," he replied. "You have to learn how to fly when you want—not just as a reflex and not just hovering."

"I told you, I don't want to fly around the city where anyone could see me, and besides, how am I supposed to practice flying without Mom and Dad finding out?"

Danny smiled again. "You leave that to me."

"Leave what to you?"

Cassie and Danny, both startled by the third voice on the roof, looked over to see their mom and dad standing in the doorway. Their mom crossed her arms. "What are we not supposed to find out, Cassie?"

4

"Mom," Cassie started, "I thought you weren't supposed to be home until eight."

"The realtor was able to get us an earlier showing," her mom replied. "What are we not supposed to find out?"

Cassie's mind went blank. She couldn't think of something fast enough. "I—uhh—Danny was—uhh—"

"I failed an English quiz," Danny finished for her. "I forgot to read a few chapters, but Mr. Hanger is going to let me retake it on Thursday. I didn't want you to find out."

Their mom's gaze narrowed, clearly disappointed, but their dad just rolled his eyes and smirked. "Failing a quiz isn't the end of the world," he said. "Just make sure you ace it on Thursday, and don't forget something like that again."

"And don't try to hide something from us again," their mom added.

"Sorry," Danny said, but Cassie could see that he was still smiling. She nudged him, and he fixed his face into a frown.

Their dad looked over at the books still sitting on the table by the bench. "Come down when you've finished your homework or at seven, whichever comes first."

"We'll be down in a little bit," Cassie said.

As their parents turned to head back downstairs to the apartment, Cassie heard her mom say, "You're too lenient with him. Failing a quiz is a big deal."

"Did you really fail a quiz?" Cassie asked Danny.

"No, it's on Thursday, and I've already read the chapters." He smiled back at her.

During dinner, Cassie was on edge. Even though her brother had promised not to tell their parents about her ability, he had a goofy smile on his face all the way through the meal. He kept looking at her as if he expected her to take off flying right there in the kitchen. Even their father seemed to sense that something else was going on.

"Why do you keep making faces at Cassie?" he asked. "What's up with you two today?"

"Nothing," Danny said, still smiling.

"He's just being a weirdo," Cassie said.

That made Danny smile even more. "Oh, *I'm* the weirdo?" he said. Cassie shot a sharp look across the table at him.

"Make sure you read those chapters before Thursday. No smiling until then," their dad said with a wink. Danny nodded and kept smiling.

After dinner, Cassie knew she should spend some time on the egg drop project, but today had just been too much. She lay down on her bed, tired and unable to shake the fear that someone might have seen her catch Danny. She might have already been discovered. Mario lived right across the street, and one of his windows faced the spot where Cassie had flown. What if he'd seen? She'd only been friends with him and Nikki for a few months now. She didn't know how they would react to something like this.

I guess there's nothing I can do about it now, she thought. *Maybe I got lucky and no one saw what happened.*

There was something else too—something she couldn't lie to herself about, no matter how hard she tried. Not only had she actually flown . . . but it had been *fun*. Shooting through the air and down the side of the building had been thrilling. It was like riding a rollercoaster that she was able to control.

Well, maybe not fully *control*, she thought. Going after Danny had just happened. She hadn't really thought about it, but something inside her said that if she wanted to, she could do the exact same thing under less extreme circumstances. She *could* fly if she wanted to.

Just before she drifted off to sleep, something occurred to her. She had been so afraid that if people found out about her ability they would think she was different, but as her body slipped into unconsciousness, she thought, *Different can also be special.*

***

"*Cassie.*" The voice was a whisper that woke her up. "*Cassie.*" It was Danny standing by her bed. "You're doing it again."

She sat up and, once again, found she was hovering several feet above the bed. Just as she realized what was happening, she dropped. "Yeah," she said to her brother as she sat up, "that's happened before."

"Come on," he said, "let's go to the roof."

"What?" Cassie said a little too loudly. "I'm not going to the roof. What time is it?"

"*Shhh,*" Danny hissed. "You'll wake up Mom and Dad. I think it's a little after midnight."

"I'm going back to sleep. We've got school tomorrow."

"I said I wouldn't tell anyone as long as you practiced flying, and you don't want to be seen, which means you can't do it in the middle of the day, so you have to do it now."

Cassie lay back down and rolled over. "Go back to bed."

"Get up," Danny urged, "or Mom and Dad find out what you can do tomorrow at breakfast."

"They wouldn't believe you," Cassie said, closing her eyes.

"Then I'll jump out the window, and you'll have to save me again. I'll do it. Don't think I won't."

Cassie opened her eyes and sat back up. "People could still see me at night. It's too risky."

Danny smiled. "I thought you might say that." He tossed something onto her lap—a black ski mask. "Put that on. No one will know who you are even if they do see you."

Cassie picked up the mask and looked at it, and then she looked at her little brother. She had to admit that would make her feel a little more comfortable with practicing her ability. "You're not going to let this go, are you?"

He smiled at her. "Nope."

She was about to tell Danny no once and for all, but then she remembered how flying had felt. There was no denying that she wanted to experience it again. Taking a deep breath, she climbed out of bed. "All right, let's do this."

5

"I look like a criminal," Cassie said. She and Danny had snuck out of their apartment and up the stairs to the roof. Before leaving, Cassie had put on some black leggings and a black shirt. It seemed like a good idea to further protect her identity, but once she put the ski mask on, she looked like she was ready to rob a bank.

"Well," Danny replied, "no one's going to know who you are. Besides, if someone sees you flying around, I don't think they'll even notice your clothes." He got that goofy grin again. "And every superhero needs a mask— Altitude wears one."

"I'm *not* some superhero," Cassie said. "But fine. So what now?"

"Now you fly."

"How?"

"How should I know? You're the one who can fly."

"This is a waste of time," Cassie said and turned to head back downstairs.

"Wait, wait, wait," Danny said, stepping in front of her to block her path, "let's start with something easy. Just try hovering. You've done it before without trying. You should be able to just do it, right?"

"Yeah, I've done it *without* trying," she said. "I don't even know where to begin doing it willingly."

"Just give it a shot," Danny said.

Cassie took a deep breath and closed her eyes. She visualized herself floating a few feet off the ground, and then, just as she had done after she caught Danny, she pushed her body upward. "Anything?" she asked.

"No," Danny replied, "you just looked like you were meditating."

Cassie threw her hands into the air. "Well, I don't know what to do then."

"Hmm," Danny said, bringing his hand to his chin and stroking the beard that wasn't there. Cassie gave him a don't-act-all-smart-with-me look, but he probably couldn't tell because of the mask. "Let's think about this. You were able to fly and get me when I fell, so maybe it's just a reflex, like you said."

"So?"

"So, we just need to do the same thing again." Danny started walking over toward the ledge where he had fallen earlier that day.

She knew what he was about to do. "Danny, don't!"

He called over his shoulder, "We know this works. It did this afternoon."

"What if it doesn't work this time?" Cassie asked. "You could get hurt, or die!"

"I don't see that happening," Danny said casually.

"Don't do it, Danny!" He had reached the ledge. "What if I can't catch you in time? This is a really bad idea!"

He was climbing up onto the ledge. "Danny, please, I'm begging you . . ."

He stood up on the ledge, turned around, and smiled at her. "Don't!" she shouted at him one more time.

"I don't have to," he said. "You're doing it."

Cassie looked down and saw that he was right. She was floating a few feet off the rooftop. She'd known it might happen, but floating without realizing it startled her. She panicked again. Her body pivoted and she ended up with her head pointed straight at the ground.

"Whoa!" Danny shouted, hopping down from the ledge back onto the rooftop and jogging over to his sister. "Relax. Try to get your feet toward the ground again."

Cassie tried to spin herself and found she was able to do so with some ease. It was a lot like being underwater. She was able to just roll herself right side up again.

"Okay," Danny said, "now try to come down slowly."

Cassie breathed deeply and tried to picture herself slowly descending back to the roof.

Instead, she just fell. It was not graceful. It was not slow. It was just a sixteen-year-old girl falling onto a rooftop. She fell into a pile. A pain shot through her ankle, and for a moment she thought she may have twisted it, but the throbbing eventually faded away. She felt a drop of blood trickle from her knee down her leg.

"Huh," Danny said, "it wasn't slow, but," he shrugged, "you did come down. We can work on that. Stand up."

"I'm not doing that again," Cassie said, rising to her feet.

"Just try to hover one more time. If you do it, we'll be done for tonight. Just try to hover once without me threatening to jump off a roof." Danny smiled at her.

"All right," she said with a sigh, "but if I do it, we're done."

"You got it," Danny said, "and this time, I'll catch you if you go too high."

Cassie took a step back from her brother and looked straight up at the sky. She had described it well before—floating really did feel like flexing a muscle. She had to concentrate fully on making her body rise up into the air, but when she looked down, she saw she was doing it. She had gone up about four feet and was still rising slowly.

"There you go!" Danny shouted excitedly to her. "You've got it!"

Suddenly, that feeling of being on a rollercoaster came rushing back to Cassie. This was thrilling. This was amazing. This was . . . getting out of hand. She was up to ten feet and still rising.

Too high, too high! she thought to herself.

"Uhh," Danny said, "you should probably start coming down now!"

She tried to stop herself, but she kept rising—twelve feet, fourteen feet. Then she reached about fifteen feet above the rooftop. She was way too high to just drop. At first her body went cold, then hot. She could feel sweat on her brow, and her chest tightened up with panic.

"I'm here to catch you," Danny whisper-shouted to her, "but just try to let yourself drift down."

"Okay," Cassie said. She tried to calm down and closed her eyes. After a moment or two, she could feel herself lowering. She opened her eyes and saw that she was, in fact, coming down slowly. Ten feet, eight feet, six feet, and when she was only three feet off the ground, she dropped onto the rooftop as if she hadn't been flying at all. She scraped her other knee and her elbow too. She would need to buy some antiseptic cream to take care of all these scrapes she was getting.

"Landings are hard," Danny said, standing over her. "We'll work on that tomorrow."

6

"A parachute would definitely be a good idea," Nikki was saying, "but I think we should give the egg some padding just in case the chute isn't enough."

"Huh?" Cassie blinked, trying to pay attention. They were sitting together in their biology classroom. All the other students were working on designs for their egg drop projects. "What were you saying?"

"I said we need padding as well as a parachute," Nikki repeated. "Are you feeling okay?"

"Yeah, yeah, I'm just tired. I didn't get much sleep last night."

"Well, this project is due in a week. I can take care of building the padding if you take care of the parachute."

"Yeah, that sounds good," Cassie said through a yawn. "I'll make the parachute."

The bell rang, signaling the end of the day. "Remember," Ms. Talin said as the students stood up and gathered their books, "along with the project on Monday, we also have a test next Friday."

"Jeez, we have so much to do next week," Nikki said. "Come on, Mario's probably already waiting for us."

Cassie glanced at Ms. Talin, who was sitting down at her desk and sifting through papers. "I'll catch up with you guys. I have to talk to Ms. Talin for a bit."

"Okay," Nikki replied, "we'll be by the flagpole when you're done."

Cassie gathered up her books and walked to the front of Ms. Talin's desk. "Ms. Talin, I— uh, I have a question."

"Go ahead," her teacher replied without looking up from her papers.

"The other day, when you dropped that weight on the egg, you said that gravity can make three pounds act like it's more than three pounds."

"That's right," Ms. Talin said. "The force of gravity gets added to the weight and makes it act as though it's more like six pounds on impact, but that depends on the height from which the weight is dropped. The higher it is, the faster it will fall when it hits the egg, up to the point of terminal velocity, that is."

She looked up from the papers. "You don't actually need to worry about the force of the weight itself, just gravity. Nothing is going to get dropped on the egg once it falls from the roof. Dropping the weight was just to demonstrate a point. Your egg will hit the ground with more force than four pounds, so you just need to lower the amount of force it lands with."

"Right," Cassie said, "but is there a way to stop the egg from hitting the ground at all?"

Ms. Talin looked confused. "What do you mean?"

"I mean, is there a way to make the egg hover in mid-air so it would never actually hit the ground? Is there a way to make gravity not work on the egg?"

"You mean make the egg resistant to Earth's gravitational pull?"

"Yeah."

Ms. Talin chuckled. "No. Gravity is a natural law. Like I said, what goes up must come down. There's no known way to conquer gravity inside the planet's atmosphere." She smiled again at Cassie. "But don't let me discourage you. If you find a way to conquer gravity, you'll definitely get an A—and probably a Nobel Prize." She paused. "Is everything all right?"

"Yeah," Cassie said, forcing her face into a smile. "Thanks."

Ms. Talin nodded, and Cassie left the room to join her friends. Mario and Nikki were still at the flagpole waiting for her. She walked down the school steps to join them.

"What did you ask Ms. Talin about?" Nikki asked as they began the walk home.

"Nothing," Cassie said. "Just had a question about the test next week."

Mario seemed to ignore what they were talking about, picking up a conversation that Cassie must have interrupted. "As I was saying, it's false advertising, I tell you! There are clear differences between chicken *nuggets* and chicken *tenders*. What they're serving us are obviously nuggets, but they're calling them tenders. There's a line, and our school has crossed it! Who's with me?"

"We're all lucky to have you defending our lunchroom rights," Nikki said with a sigh. "Our school superhero."

"Injustice cannot stand," he said and struck a dramatic pose with his hands on his hips.

"Hey," Cassie said suddenly, "what would you guys do if you found out you actually had superpowers?"

"Start making an awesome costume," Mario fired back.

"It would depend on what superpower I had," Nikki said.

"Let's say you could fly," Cassie said.

"Like Altitude?" Mario asked. "The first thing I'd do is fly to Australia, grab a koala, and bring it back to my house. Then, I'd probably go to Antarctica and grab a penguin. Ooooh, I've always wanted a pet panda, so next I'd go to—"

"Honestly," Nikki interrupted, "I'd probably keep it to myself, not use it unless I had to."

"Seriously?" Mario turned to her and threw up his hands in the air. "What a waste! You're telling me you really wouldn't fly, even if you could?"

"No," she said matter-of-factly. "Think of what could happen if everyone knew there was someone who could fly. People would want to experiment on you—or worse, use you as a spy. Everyone who needed their cat out of a tree or their ball off a roof would be calling constantly. Plus, you'd probably turn into a celebrity."

"And that's bad, why?" Mario asked.

"I don't want to be famous," Nikki replied, shrugging. "Too much pressure. What about you, Cass?"

"I honestly don't know what I'd do," she said quietly.

They'd reached the street where Nikki made a left and Mario and Cassie kept going straight. Nikki said goodbye, and the other two continued together.

"I can't believe she wouldn't use her power if she could fly," Mario said.

Cassie shrugged. "She's got a point. There are a lot of drawbacks."

Mario stopped walking. "Drawbacks? Who cares about the drawbacks? If I could fly, I would use it *for sure*! Yeah, people would be calling to get cats out of trees and stuff, but that's because they need help. Besides, it wouldn't just be that kind of little problem all the time. There would be people who really needed someone who could fly. If you could and didn't help people in need, that's way worse than any of your little drawbacks."

Cassie smiled at him. "Yeah, I guess you're kind of right." They continued walking home while Mario listed off what other animals he would take home if he could fly.

The apartment was empty as usual. Cassie went into her room and pulled the ski mask out of the back of the closet where she had thrown it after the flying lesson the night before. She considered tossing it back in, but instead, she laid it out on her desk. She'd use it again tonight.

7

For the next week, every night Danny would
sneak into Cassie's room and wake her up
to practice flying. She'd put on her ski mask
and, under the cover of darkness, she began
by hovering above the roof of her apartment
building.

The first night, Danny told her to hover as
high up as she was comfortable with, holding
it for as long as she possibly could. Cassie
still didn't understand how she was able to
accomplish this.

Maybe I will get a Nobel Prize, she thought to
herself while she was suspended in midair.

On her first attempt, she was able to hover

for a full five minutes before she crashed to the ground, leaving her with a nasty scrape on her forearm. It took incredible concentration to hover, and the second that concentration was broken, she fell to the ground.

"Ughh, I'm never going to get this," she said.

"Altitude didn't get it right away either," Danny replied, playing up the wise instructor act. "He kept trying until he did."

On her second attempt, she hovered for eight minutes, and while she tried to land softly, she crashed again, this time twisting her wrist. "I've got to work on those landings," she said to Danny, who was eating chips on the bench and offering encouraging words every few minutes.

"Altitude comes swooping in when he lands," Danny offered. "Once he's about a foot off the ground, he just lets himself fall naturally, but he always lands on his feet."

"Yeah, but when I'm coming down, it's like my ability cuts off or something." She stood up. "I don't know what my problem is."

"Go for ten minutes this time," Danny suggested.

Cassie yawned. "I don't know. I'm tired."

"If you can figure this out when you're tired," Danny said, "imagine what you'll be able to do when you're not tired."

Cassie tried to shake the sleepiness out of her head and prepared to take off again. "Ten minutes?"

"Ten minutes," Danny said, stuffing another handful of chips in his mouth.

She took off. Each time she did it, it got a little easier. This time she lifted off the ground right away. When she reached ten feet in the air, she stopped—another skill that was coming easier and easier each time she flew. She closed her eyes and focused only on floating, staying exactly where she was. She didn't think about the ground or about the fact that, this high up, if she blew the landing again she could really hurt herself. While she was in the air, she only thought about staying there. Nothing else mattered in that moment. The rest of the world faded away.

"I think you can come down now," Danny said eventually.

"Was that ten minutes?" Cassie asked.

"No," Danny replied. "It was twenty."

She tried to focus on coming down, and at first she descended slowly, but at five feet off the ground, she dropped like a rock. This time she anticipated the fall and managed to avoid hurting herself, but it still wasn't graceful.

The next night, the two snuck up onto the roof just like the night before, only this time Danny brought a handful of candy bars to munch on. He had her start by hovering for a few minutes, but when she crashed to the ground, he said, "That was just a warm up. See if you can start hovering over there," he pointed to the corner of the roof, "and float over to me."

Cassie walked over to the spot Danny had chosen. She rose eight feet into the air. That part was easy now. She looked at Danny, who was watching her expectantly, and she tried to move over to him. At first, she didn't move at all, just hung in the air, but she tried again, focusing all her energy on pushing her way toward her brother. This time, she started inching forward.

As soon as she started moving, she felt an incredible rush. She couldn't help but start laughing with joy even though she was going more slowly than her average walking pace. It still felt better than anything she had ever experienced.

She made it over to her brother and didn't even try to stick the landing this time. She crashed to the ground, but if she hurt herself, she didn't feel it because she was so excited about what she'd just done.

"Did you see that?" she shouted to Danny.

"I saw it," Danny said, flatly.

"I totally did it!" Cassie said, holding her hands to her head and walking in circles. "I actually flew!"

"Yeah, you did," Danny said, standing up from the bench, "but you could have been outrun by a turtle driving a broken go-kart. I know you can go faster—I've seen you do it. See if you can float back a little quicker."

Cassie did it again and again, floating from one end of the roof to the other, over and over. By the time they were done for the night, she was able to drift a little faster than she could walk. She still wasn't nailing her landings—she was going through more packs of bandages and antiseptic than she'd ever thought possible— but she was making incredible progress.

8

School was becoming difficult to sit through. Not only were the late nights taking a toll on her, but all Cassie could think about during class was flying. English, math, biology—it didn't matter. She'd sit in her desk and think about hovering over her apartment rooftop. Half the time, she didn't hear a word her teachers were saying.

"Have you finished the parachute?" Nikki asked during lunch one day.

"What?" Cassie had spaced out while looking at the tacos on her lunch tray. She could barely keep her eyes open.

"The parachute—have you finished it?"

"What parachute?"

Nikki rolled her eyes. "For the egg drop! You need to make a parachute so the egg will land safely. The project is due on Monday."

"Right," Cassie said. "Yeah, sorry. I'll get it done over the weekend."

Now Cassie remembered the plan for the egg drop. Nikki had built a cube full of dozens of rubber bands. The egg would be suspended inside the cube, cushioned by the rubber bands to soften the impact. Cassie's job was to make a parachute that could slow the fall of the half-pound cube (egg included) as much as possible.

"What's going on with you?" Nikki asked.

"Yeah," Mario added, "why do you look so tired all the time, and what's with all the scrapes—"

"I'm fine," Cassie replied a little too quickly. "Seriously. I just—I just tripped while I was up on the roof."

"The roof?" Nikki asked. "What were you doing up there?"

Cassie felt her face flush. "Nothing," she said. "My little brother likes going up there."

Mario and Nikki exchanged a suspicious glance but didn't press any further. At least for the moment.

***

That night, she flew again. Taking off was a breeze now, and floating from one location to another had gotten easier and easier. Danny would shout directions to her, and she would follow his instructions. After successfully moving all over the roof, she began to fly out over the street, just past the edge of the building. Cassie was nervous about it the first time, but after five or six repetitions, she flew confidently over a ten story drop. There was only one problem: she was never able to land the way she wanted. She fell every time.

Without school the next day, Cassie's practice could go much later Friday and Saturday nights. She spent most of Saturday afternoon practically pacing in her bedroom, anxiously waiting for the sun to go down.

That night after dinner, she sat in the living room with her parents, watching TV.

Her phone buzzed on the coffee table. It was a text from Nikki in their group message with Mario: *Movie tonight?*

Can't, she typed back. She looked around the room, trying to come up with something for an excuse. Her eyes landed on her backpack, sitting in the same spot it had been since she got home Friday afternoon. *I have a ton of homework.*

Boooo! Mario texted in response.

She felt a little guilty but didn't bother replying, knowing the more excuses she gave, the more suspicious she would seem. Glancing at the clock to see how much time had passed while she was texting with Mario and Nikki, she frowned. It had barely been five minutes.

Cassie made a point of yawning loudly over the next few hours. Seeing her yawn never failed to make her dad yawn too. Before long, he announced he was tired and headed to bed. Then her mom turned in too.

Cassie waited another hour before heading up to the roof with Danny.

By the end of the weekend, Cassie felt that she was close to mastering her power.

She could hover on command without much concentration. She could float to wherever Danny directed her. She'd even started doing tricks, going in loops and spirals, just to see if she could do it. She was feeling more confident with her ability than ever, and the rush that she got when she first floated on command never seemed to go away. It was thrilling every time. *If only I could learn how to land,* she thought, *I'd be pretty much perfect.*

Sunday night's practice was the best yet. Cassie was confident, and Danny wasn't even giving her directions anymore. He'd fallen asleep on the bench while Cassie flew around in the air above her apartment building, zipping this way, then that way, stopping in midair just to start again. She woke up on Monday morning exhausted but with a big smile. Nothing could bring her down today.

"Where's the parachute?" Nikki asked as Cassie opened her locker to grab the books for her first class.

"You missed a pretty good movie, by the way," Mario said, standing right behind Nikki.

Cassie felt her heart fall into her stomach. The egg drop challenge was today, and she'd completely forgotten the project. Nikki had been counting on her. Cassie stood there, holding her locker door with her mouth slightly open, unable to say anything, even apologize.

"You told us you had too much homework to hang out this weekend," Nikki said, crossing her arms. "What were you actually doing all weekend?"

"I was—I just—" Cassie's brain felt like it was working in slow motion. She couldn't think of anything to say that could make this better.

"Forget it," Nikki snapped.

"I'm sorry."

Nikki didn't say anything. Instead, she turned around and walked away.

Cassie didn't know what to do. She looked at Mario for support. He offered a little half-smile, but he shook his head. "See you at lunch," he said, following after Nikki.

Cassie stayed at her locker, staring at nothing and feeling awful until the first bell rang.

9

Ms. Talin led all the students up through
a stairwell and onto the roof. Each pair of
students presented their contraption to the
teacher before dropping it off the three story
building. Nikki refused to even look at Cassie
as egg after egg landed safely on the ground
below.

Most of the other teams were successful.
The students high-fived and cheered after their
successes. The more eggs stayed intact, the
more nervous Cassie got. She was sweating and
couldn't stop fidgeting.

When it was their turn, Cassie and Nikki
stepped forward and handed the cube that

Nikki had made to Ms. Talin. The teacher gave the device a skeptical look, as if she could tell it was incomplete, and handed it back to Nikki.

As her friend approached the edge of the building, Cassie was so nervous that she felt herself start to float a few inches off the ground. She quickly concentrated and landed. A quick glance around confirmed that no one had seen her.

CRACK. The cube shattered and the inside of the egg splattered all over the sidewalk. Some of the other students winced, watching the failure. Ms. Talin shook her head and made a mark on a clipboard. Cassie gave an apologetic look to Nikki, but her friend still wouldn't look at her.

There was only one other team whose egg broke. Cassie could tell from Nikki's tense expression that she wasn't happy to be one of the only unsuccessful teams.

Once all the eggs had dropped, the class returned from the roof to the classroom. Ms. Talin explained why some eggs had broken while others had survived. Cassie was relieved when the bell rang for the end of the day, concluding her embarrassment.

"Nikki," she started, but Nikki wordlessly gathered her books and avoided eye contact with her. "Nikki, I'm sorry. Please—"

Nikki stopped, sighed, and then turned to look at Cassie.

"I'll talk to Ms. Talin and tell her this is my fault, that I forgot to do my share of the project. Maybe she'll let us redo it." Nikki was quiet, considering this.

"I'm so sorry I forgot," Cassie added. "Will you and Mario wait for me by the flagpole?"

"Fine," Nikki said, turning to head out the door and not looking back.

***

At the flagpole, Mario was staring at his phone while Nikki kicked some rocks around the pavement. Cassie ran up to them.

"Ms. Talin said we could redo the project on Wednesday," she said to Nikki. "I told her it was my fault that we weren't ready."

Nikki nodded. "Okay," she said. "I can make another cube, probably better this time."

"I'm so sorry I forgot. I won't let you down again."

Nikki scrunched her face up in confusion. "What's been going on with you? You're forgetting projects. You look like you haven't slept in days, and you're covered in scratches. Is something wrong?"

"I've just been feeling a little under the weather lately," she said.

Mario cocked an eyebrow. "What sickness gives you scratches like that?"

"No," she said, "that's—that's unrelated."

Mario rolled his eyes. "If you don't want to tell us, don't tell us, but you're acting weird, Cass."

She felt the panic set in—the whole point in keeping her flying a secret was so people didn't think she was weird, and here she was, being weird by being so secretive. "I—I know I haven't been a very good friend lately—"

"No, you haven't," Nikki said. "Look, we get if something is going on with you that you can't talk to us about, but that doesn't mean you can flake out on us either. If you need some space, just say so."

Mario nodded. "Yeah, or you *can* talk to us about it."

Cassie gave them a tight smile. "I can't—it's not really something I can talk about." Mario and Nikki exchanged a glance. "I'm working on it," she said.

Nikki raised her eyebrows at that but said nothing. She started the walk home and the other two followed in silence. Cassie got to her apartment, went into her room, tossed her bag next to her desk, and lay down on the bed.

What am I doing? she thought to herself. *I want to keep flying, but I let Nikki down. And I can't keep functioning with so little sleep. I've got to take a break from flying and make sure the rest of my life doesn't fall apart.*

Cassie considered telling her friends what she could do—why she had seemed so off her game recently. Her parents had believed that the scratches came from playing field hockey in PE, but that wouldn't work on Mario and

Nikki. They knew that PE was focused on volleyball right now.

She needed to get her life back in order, and for now that meant concentrating on school, getting enough sleep each night, and being there for her friends. She wouldn't use her power until she'd gotten a handle on everything, so there was no reason to tell them now. Maybe she would later.

She sat down at her desk and pulled some cloth out of an old sewing kit. Cutting a large octagon out of it, she began fashioning a parachute for their egg. She wouldn't disappoint Nikki again.

"Cass?" Danny was home.

"I'm in here," she shouted back, not looking up from her task.

Danny pushed the door open. "So what do you want to practice tonight?"

"Nothing," Cassie replied sharply. Danny flinched at the response. "I'm not flying anymore—or at least for a while."

"Why? What happened?"

"I failed a project. I completely forgot to

do my part for it, and I almost got Nikki in trouble too."

Danny nodded. "Okay."

Cassie looked up from the parachute, surprised. "Okay?" She had expected him to put up a fight, to push her to fly more.

"Yeah, I get it," Danny said again. "You can't stop paying attention to everything else in your life just because you can fly. I didn't know practicing was this hard on you. Besides," he shrugged, "you're as good as Altitude now. Your training is complete."

Cassie couldn't help but chuckle. Her little brother was acting like he had just finished teaching her karate. "Thanks, Danny."

He held up a finger. "I have something I want to give you." He disappeared from her door, and she heard him rummaging around in his own room before he appeared again. He was holding something shiny and gold. "I want you to have this."

She took it out of his hand and turned it over. It was a set of gold wings that Danny had gotten from a flight attendant the first time they'd been on an airplane as a family. For years, the trinket had been a prized possession, proudly displayed on top of his dresser. As he'd gotten older, the wings fell out of favor. Cassie was surprised to see he still had them. "Seems like a better fit for *you* now," he said with a small smile.

Cassie hugged her little brother. "Thank you, Danny." He smiled back at her before heading to the living room to watch TV. He wasn't supposed to do that before finishing his homework, but Cassie let him anyway.

She got back to work on her project. In her mind, she kept repeating, *No more flying. No more flying. No more flying.*

The more she thought it to herself, the worse it sounded. *I was meant to fly. I must have been, or I wouldn't be able to.*

Then she remembered Nikki and how close she'd come to ruining their project, and her thoughts returned to: *No more flying. No more flying. No more flying.*

Just before bed, Cassie went into her closet and pulled out the black shirt that she'd worn during her flying practices. She gently pinned the wings to the shirt and placed it back in the closet. Just before she fell asleep, she thought to herself, *No more flying.*

10

Two days later, after the final bell, Nikki and Cassie went up to the roof of the school with Ms. Talin to redo their egg drop assignment. The cube, with the parachute attached, worked perfectly. The egg landed gently on the sidewalk below.

"Well done, girls," Ms. Talin said. "Nikki, you will get full credit, and Cassie, you'll get half credit."

"Thank you, Ms. Talin," they both replied, though Nikki looked at Cassie in surprise.

As usual, they met Mario at the flagpole once they were done. He was sitting on the sidewalk playing a hand-held video game.

When he saw them coming, he stood up. "How'd it go?"

"Our egg survived," Cassie said with a relieved sigh.

Nikki turned to Cassie. "I didn't know you would only get half credit."

She shrugged. "It was my fault the project wasn't done on time. I told Ms. Talin it wasn't fair for you to get punished for my mistake."

Nikki smiled. "Well, thanks."

As the three of them walked home, Nikki and Mario joked with each other about something, but Cassie wasn't paying attention. She was thinking about flying, something she hadn't let herself do since failing the first egg drop, even though she'd wanted to. For the last few nights, she'd had trouble falling asleep because she felt such a temptation to sneak up onto the roof and take off.

Maybe just for a little bit, she'd think to herself while lying in bed. Then, *No, not until I get my school work back in order.*

Now that her science project was finished, she considered sneaking out tonight.

At home, she found a note on the refrigerator, saying that her parents would be out late again tonight, looking at a house.

I finished the egg drop project, she thought. *Haven't I earned a night of flying?* Then she remembered she had a history test coming up in a few days. She hadn't studied at all yet. *No, I can't fly yet—not until I get a handle on this stuff.*

Cassie sat down at her desk and tried to focus on homework, but every few minutes she found herself staring at the closet, thinking about the mask and the black shirt with the wings pinned to it. *No, not yet*, she reminded herself again.

"Cass?" Danny was home. She got off her bed and went out of her room to greet him.

"Hey, Danny," she said. "Mom and Dad left a note—they have another house showing. They'll be back at eight."

"Don't suppose you want to go fly for a bit?"

Cassie shook her head. "No, not until I'm feeling better about school. Besides, it's still light out and I don't want anyone to see me."

Danny still didn't push her. Instead, he nodded as if he understood. "Well, can we go up on the roof anyway? I'll just do my homework, I promise."

"You're not going to jump off the roof again?"

"No," he said. "But it's nice to know I could," he added with a smile.

They both grabbed their bags and headed upstairs. Danny worked diligently on his homework, rarely looking up from his books. He didn't go anywhere near the ledge. Cassie, on the other hand, had trouble focusing. She'd start reading a paragraph or begin a math problem, only to space out and look at the ledge of the roof, wanting so badly to jump over it and fly. She had to keep reminding herself to concentrate.

Don't think about flying, she thought, *at least for now, maybe a week, and if I'm feeling like I've got everything else under control, maybe I'll start again.*

Hours went by and Cassie had gotten less done than she'd hoped. She had finished most of her other assignments but still hadn't started studying for her history test. It was getting dark and cold, plus Danny was hungry, so they left the roof and went back to the apartment to get dinner out of the fridge. Once they were done eating, Cassie took out her history book and sat down to read the assigned chapters, but she fell asleep, book in hand, after about an hour. Immediately, she was flying. She could at least still use her ability in dreams. At first, she soared over buildings, then descended and began whipping around corners with speed and precision. She went as fast as she could, enjoying the sensation even though she was aware it was just a dream. It was as close as she could get right now.

"Cassie!"

Her eyes shot open at the sound of Danny yelling. The air coming in through the open windows smelled odd, like something had burned in the oven.

"Cassie, wake up!"

"I'm awake—I'm awake!" she said rubbing the sleep out of her eyes. *Is someone shouting outside?* "What's wrong?"

Danny pointed to the window. "There's a fire!"

"What? Where?"

"Mario's building!"

Cassie got off the couch and ran to the window. Flames and smoke were shooting out of the windows in the first three floors of Mario's apartment building. Mario lived on the sixth floor, and Cassie could see that his window was open, but smoke was pouring out of it.

No fire trucks had arrived yet, but many of the building's residents as well as some onlookers had assembled in the street outside to watch the blaze. Cassie scanned the crowd for Mario. She couldn't find him. Then she saw his parents. They were in the middle of the street, frantically pointing at the building.

Cassie gasped. *Mario's still inside.*

11

"You have to do something!" Danny shouted.

"What am I supposed to do? I'm not a firefighter!" Cassie snapped, pacing back and forth in the apartment.

"The window is open! You can get in there!"

Cassie went over to the window again. She hoped she would see Mario come running down the street, wondering what all the commotion was outside his building, but he didn't. His parents were still shouting at anyone who would listen.

"Cassie, you have to do something." She knew Danny was right.

She ran to her room and grabbed the ski mask out of her closet—no time for the black shirt and pants. She covered her face as she ran up the stairs to the roof. From there, she could still see Mario's apartment window. Danny followed her up.

"Hurry!" he said, and just before she took off he added, "Good luck!"

It wasn't a challenge to lift off the ground, not at all like when she started flying. Instincts took over, and she lifted off with ease. She aimed for Mario's open window and flew forward as quickly as she could.

She moved faster than she had expected, even more rapidly than when she had caught Danny falling off the roof. As she soared easily through the window, she heard sirens in the distance. The firefighters were coming, but she didn't know if they would make it in time to get Mario out of the apartment.

The apartment was filled with smoke. It billowed around quickly, scorching Cassie's lungs and mouth as she breathed. She dropped to the floor to avoid inhaling as much as she could, but it wasn't much better. The whole apartment was hot.

"Mario!" she called out, but shouting made her cough and she didn't hear if there was a response. "Mario!" she tried again, this time covering her mouth and stifling the urge to hack up the smoke.

Over the high-pitched wail of the fire alarm, she heard it—groaning. It was coming from near the front door. Cassie army-crawled toward the sound. When she got a little closer, she saw a heap on the floor.

She crawled over to Mario and shouted his name, but he was unconscious. Cassie got her arms under him and tried to lift, but she wasn't strong enough to get him off the ground. He wasn't waking up from her shouting in his ear either. She knew the more time he spent in the smoke-filled apartment, the more toxic fumes he would inhale. She had to get him out of here somehow.

She tried lifting him again, but he was too heavy. Her arms might not have been strong enough to lift her friend, but maybe her superhuman ability was. She got her arms under his with his back to her chest, and this time, instead of trying to lift him, she closed her eyes and concentrated as hard as she could on levitating. When she opened her eyes, she was a few feet off the ground, and Mario was lifting with her. His feet were still dragging along the floor, but her plan was working—she could float him out of here.

Cassie pivoted away from the door, desperate to get him to safety. The window she had entered through seemed too far away now, and the smoke was building up on that side of the apartment. She looked around and saw another open window, one that faced the alleyway between Mario's building and the one next to it.

She focused all her energy on moving Mario out through the alleyway window. Progress was slow. They barely moved at all at first, but the closer they got, the faster Cassie was able to go. When they reached the window, Cassie struggled to levitate a little higher just to get out. *Just a few inches more.*

She and Mario slowly drifted out the open window between the buildings, but they were still six stories off the ground. Now, she focused entirely on coming down slowly—which was much harder with Mario's weight pulling her downward. It felt like trying to float slowly to the bottom of a pool with a sack of bricks tied to her ankle. She was concentrating so hard that her face scrunched up and she could feel sweat coming out of every pore on her body, but it was working. They were coming down.

Cassie was focusing so hard about not letting them simply drop the entire six stories that she didn't notice Mario's eyes open as his head drifted back onto her shoulder. "Cass?" he mumbled. "What's happening?"

The words caught her by such surprise that she momentarily lost her focus, and they dropped a full story before she steadied herself.

"Mario, you're okay!" She didn't know how he'd recognized her with the ski mask covering her face.

"What's going on? Where are we?"

"We're in the alleyway next to your building. Don't worry—you're safe."

Mario looked down through bloodshot and groggy eyes. "Are we flying?"

They dropped a little faster as Cassie lost her focus again. "No—no, you're, uh, you're imagining things."

They were seven feet off the ground when Cassie, once again, failed to make a graceful landing. They fell in a heap.

"Mario, are you okay?" Cassie asked, but he had fallen unconscious again. She rolled him over and tried to pick him up to take him out to the street. The alleyway was filled with smoke, and Cassie wanted to get him out of there as fast as possible. She couldn't lift him, and she didn't want to risk floating with him into the street where anyone could see her flying.

Even though Mario was unconscious, Cassie said, "I'll be right back." She pulled off the mask and stuffed it into a back pocket as she ran out into the street. The fire department had arrived on the scene, so Cassie grabbed the first firefighter she saw and brought him back with her to retrieve Mario.

The firefighter lifted him up as if he weighed nothing, took him out into the street, and loaded his unconscious body into the back of a waiting ambulance while Cassie retrieved his parents. As the ambulance drove away, Cassie looked around and felt a sudden rush of panic. There were so many people in the street. It was unlikely that her flight had gone unseen. Even though she was wearing a mask while she flew, if anyone had seen her they could easily recognize that she was still wearing the same clothes. Someone here now probably knew what she could do. Mario almost certainly did.

She looked up at the top of her building. There was Danny waiting and watching from the roof. She had to head back inside and clean up before her parents got home. Once that was done, all she could do was hope that her secret was still safe.

12

Cassie and Nikki went to the hospital to visit Mario the day after the fire, but he was asleep when they got there. The doctors said he had inhaled a lot of smoke and he needed rest, but that he'd probably be ready to return to school in a few days. His parents promised they would call if anything happened.

In the meantime, Cassie had never felt so tense in her life. Every time someone said her name, she expected it to be followed by, "I know your secret." She dreaded leaving her apartment, afraid someone who'd witnessed the fire would point at her and say, "That's the flying girl!" loudly enough for everyone to hear.

Days passed, but nothing happened. She even did well on her history test. The more time went on, the less likely it seemed that someone had seen her fly. Even her parents, who talked to all of their neighbors about the fire, never mentioned anything about someone flying into the burning building. She started to think she was safe, but there was still Mario. He'd woken up during Cassie's rescue. He had even asked if they were flying. If he remembered any of it, her secret was blown, and she had no idea what he would think of her then.

Once he had been released from the hospital with a clean bill of health, Cassie tried to call Mario. He answered but said he didn't have time to talk. He and his parents were busy getting settled into a family friend's home until they figured out what to do.

When she finally did see him at school, Mario was strolling down the hallway toward her. She took a deep breath and prepared for the worst, for him to confront her about what she'd done, for him to ask if she could fly.

"Hey," he said.

"Hey," she replied. "You're feeling better I take it?"

"Yeah," he said with a smile. "Apparently, I owe you a thank you."

Cassie felt every muscle in her body go rigid all at once. "For what?"

"For saving me."

"I didn't save you," she lied in a last-ditch effort.

Mario looked at her like she just told him that one plus one equals cactus. "Yes, you did. The firefighters told me. I was in the alley, and they said you told them where to find me. They rescued me because of you."

Cassie's entire body relaxed. "Oh. Right." She couldn't help herself from smiling with relief.

He gave her a confused look but shook it off. "Anyway, I got you something." He reached into his backpack, pulled out a book, and handed it to her.

She read the title aloud: *"Humans and Superpowers: The Chosen Few."* Her stomach dropped again. *Wait, what?* Did he actually know?

"Remember a while back when you asked what we'd do if we had superpowers? That book is really good if you're interested in that kind of thing. I read it while I was in the hospital." He paused. "I don't remember a lot about the fire, but there was something, a hazy kind of memory—"

"You're back!" Nikki shouted suddenly as she ran up to Mario and gave him a big hug.

"I am," he said. "Thanks to Cass."

Nikki turned to Cassie. "What?"

The bell rang. Mario shook his head. "I'll tell you at lunch. Save a seat for me," he said as he walked away.

Nikki gave a confused look to Cassie. "What did he mean?"

Cassie couldn't think of a lie fast enough, so she just said, "I have to get to class," and rushed off.

The hours until lunch dragged on. It was only a matter of time before Mario revealed that he knew she could fly, and what made it worse was that he was apparently going to say so in front of Nikki. She imagined the two of them immediately wanting to end their friendship with her because of this—or worse, maybe they would tell everyone that she was a freak. When the bell rang for lunch after Cassie's history class, she didn't get up right away. She sat there, trying to gather her thoughts and prepare herself. It wasn't until her teacher asked if Cassie was all right that she made a speedy exit.

After picking up her lunch in the line, she walked through the cafeteria and saw Mario and Nikki sitting at their usual table. She took a deep breath and walked over.

"Well hey there, hero," Nikki said the moment Cassie sat down.

"I'm not a hero," she said flatly.

"Mario said you were the one who showed the firefighters where to find him in that alley. Who knows what would have happened if you hadn't been there."

He must not have told Nikki yet. Unable to think of anything to say, Cassie began to eat her lunch even though she wasn't hungry.

Mario looked at Cassie and gave her a strange smile before he said, "What did I miss in English?"

"Not much," Nikki said. "We have to read five chapters . . ."

Cassie stopped listening. Mario seemed to have moved on with their conversation. *Maybe I overreacted,* she thought, staring down at her lunch as she stirred it around with her fork. *Maybe he really doesn't remember what happened.* Cassie let out a silent sigh of relief.

The rest of the day passed without the dread Cassie had been feeling that morning. She went to the rest of her classes and walked home with her two best friends the way she always had. The only other mention of the fire was Mario telling them that he was most disappointed that his video games had been damaged.

When Danny got home, Cassie couldn't resist telling him what had happened that day. "I was so worried that he'd figured it out, but I guess I just panicked for no reason," she sighed. "Seems like the he's dropped the subject now."

Danny shook his head and said, "Maybe you should tell them."

"What do you mean?"

"I mean they're your friends," Danny said. "They're not going to treat you like a freak, and if you want to keep the secret from the rest of the world, Mario's obviously not going to say anything if he knows you don't want him to. The same thing goes for Nikki—and Mom and Dad."

Cassie crossed her arms, uncertain. "It's just—the fewer people who know, the better."

Danny shook his head again. "You're not going to be able to keep the secret forever. Eventually, someone's going to find out. And when that happens, I think you'll feel a lot better about it if you know you've got people you can trust." He picked up his bag, went into his room, and quietly closed the door.

At first, Cassie thought her brother was wrong—she *could* keep this secret forever. She'd done pretty well so far, hadn't she?

Still, there was some truth to what he'd said. It was likely that someone would find out unless Cassie was on guard at every moment. The more she thought about it, the more exhausting the idea of keeping this secret by herself seemed.

Later that night, Danny's words kept rolling over in her mind. She hadn't decided what to do yet when she fell into a restless sleep. Sometime around three in the morning, she woke. It didn't scare her this time. She knew what was happening—she was floating above her bed again. She realized that at any moment, her parents could walk into her room and see her floating. Sooner or later, they would find out. And then they'd feel betrayed because she'd kept such a big secret from them. They wouldn't understand what was going on—and they'd probably be as panicked as she had been back when this all started. It wouldn't be fair of her to put them through that, to keep the people who cared about her in the dark, until they accidentally saw something that confused and scared them.

She had to tell them.

13

Once again, Cassie found herself on edge during school. Today was the day that her whole life was going to change. That morning at breakfast, she had asked her parents if it was okay for Mario and Nikki to come over for dinner. For once, they didn't have any house showings.

Cassie ran into Nikki at school first. Just asking Nikki to come over that night made her nervous, but also relieved. At least this was going to be the end of keeping a secret from the people who meant most to her.

At lunch, she and Mario sat down at their usual table before Nikki got there. When Cassie asked him if he wanted to have dinner with her family, he asked, "What's the occasion?"

"You'll see when you get there."

Mario cocked an eyebrow. "Does this have anything to do with the fact that I have fuzzy memories of you in a ski mask taking me out of my burning building?" He asked it so matter-of-factly that it caught Cassie off guard.

"What? I—uhh—"

Mario held up a hand. "It's all right. After I was in the hospital for a bit, I pieced it together. That fuzzy memory, the weird stuff that's been going on with you—I'm not stupid, Cass."

"How did you know?"

"Because you were the one who showed the firefighter where to find me in the alley."

"So? Who says I didn't just find you there?"

"Well," Mario said, "how did I get there in the first place? I remember being in the apartment, and I remember choking on the smoke, then I've got all these hazy memories of you wearing a ski mask and carrying me. Next thing I know, I'm being carried by a firefighter to an ambulance."

"You probably took the fire escape."

"Yeah, that's what I thought too. Then I remembered that the fire escape is on the other side of the building," he said with a smirk. "Unless I jumped out the window, fell six stories, and managed not to break any bones, you had something to do with me being down there."

Cassie opened her mouth to reply, but she didn't know what to say.

"But," he continued, leaning back in his seat, "I'm guessing tonight I'll get to figure out how you did that, huh?"

She smiled. "Yeah, I guess you will."

When Danny got home, Cassie explained her plan to tell Mario, Nikki, and their parents. He dropped his backpack, threw his hands into the air, and groaned, "Finally!" Then he hugged her and assured her that everything would be all right.

"In fact," he said, "things are going to be better than all right. You know how I've helped you keep this secret for so long?"

Cassie nodded.

"Well, now there'll be four other people who can help you keep it secret if you want. You're making the right decision."

***

That night, as soon as the family sat down to dinner with Nikki and Mario, Cassie's mom asked why she had arranged this gathering.

"I'll get to that after dinner," said Cassie.

"Why can't you just tell us now?" Nikki asked.

"Just let her show you after dinner," Danny chimed in.

"He knows!" their dad shouted, pointing with his fork. "He knows what it is, and he's not telling us."

Everyone started eating a lot faster, and when they had all finished, Cassie asked them to head up to the roof. She went into her room and grabbed the ski mask, which still smelled like smoke from the fire. When she got up to the roof, her friends and family were standing in a group.

"All right, Cass," her dad said, "we're all up here. What is it that you wanted to show us?"

"Something I can do," she replied and put the mask over her head.

"Is that really necessary?" her mom asked.

"Yes, I don't want anyone to know what I can do other than the people on this roof right now."

Her dad shook his head. "Okay, so what is it that you can do?"

"This." And she took off.

ONE YEAR LATER

FIFTEEN SAVED DURING BRIDGE DISASTER

Fourteen civilians and one maintenance worker were saved yesterday when a bridge collapsed, trapping them between burning wreckage and a twenty-story drop into the river. The rescued people report that a mysterious, masked teenage girl came to their rescue. According to sources, she flew each of them to safe ground.

The chief of police has yet to comment on the existence of a girl with the power of flight, but this incident marks the sixth report this year of this unique individual helping at the scene of an emergency. The only distinguishing feature of the girl is reported to be a gold wing pin on her shirt. All fifteen survivors of the bridge collapse, though they do not know her name, send their sincerest gratitude to their hero.

...G A SUPERPOWER IS NOT ...

...HE COMIC BOOKS MAKE IT

...CK OUT ALL OF THE TITLES

SUPER
HUMAN

SERIES

...D OVER MATTER   STRETCHED TOO...

...U YOU SEE ME   STRONGHOL...

...KING UP SPEED   TAKE TO THE S...

ABOUT THE AUTHOR

R. T. Martin lives in St. Paul, Minnesota. When he is not drinking coffee or writing, he is busy thinking about drinking coffee and writing.